CUMBRIA LIBRARIES

3 8003 05187 9773

KT-151-641

This Little Tiger book
belongs to:

_____

_____

_____

To my husband Philip, because regular princes are boring ~ A B

To Pepin, for loving me unconditionally.
You are my favourite furry beast ~ S S

LITTLE TIGER PRESS LTD,
an imprint of the Little Tiger Group
1 Coda Studios, 189 Munster Road,
London SW6 6AW
www.littletiger.co.uk

First published in Great Britain 2018
This edition published 2019
Text copyright © Anna Bowles 2018
Illustrations copyright © Sara Sanchez 2018
Anna Bowles and Sara Sanchez have
asserted their rights to be identified as
the author and illustrator of this work under
the Copyright, Designs and Patents Act, 1988

A CIP catalogue record for this book is
available from the British Library
All rights reserved

ISBN 978-1-78881-334-1
Printed in China
LTP/1400/2594/1218
4 6 8 10 9 7 5 3

FAIRYTALE CLASSICS

Beauty and the Beast

Anna Bowles

Sara Sanchez

LITTLE TIGER
LONDON

Once upon a time . . .

there was a **family** with SIX children.

They all had **different** hobbies.

This got quite **expensive** for their parents.

Luckily, their father was a **rich** merchant.

Well, quite rich.

Well, a bit rich.

Oh dear.

The entire family had to sell **everything**
they owned and move to a tiny cottage in the woods.

Beauty's father went into town to try
to make money, but he had no luck.
As he rode back, poor and alone,
he had to take shelter in a castle.

There he found delicious food and a cosy place
to rest. Yet the castle seemed to have no owner.

As he left the next morning, the merchant picked a rose from the castle's garden to take to his daughter, Beauty.

bellowed the Beast.

"U-um . . ." stammered the merchant. "I didn't think
one flower would be a problem . . ."

"I will let you go on this condition," said the Beast.
"You must send one of your daughters to live with me. I won't
eat her, as long as she's not the one with the trombone."

The merchant went home to fetch Beauty. She was very upset, but understood she had to go.

"Welcome to your new home, Beauty," said the Beast.
She looked at him. He was huge. And very hairy.
But although she was scared inside, she didn't show it.
The Beast smiled.

The Beast had prepared a wonderful bedroom
for Beauty. But she missed her father so much
that she barely noticed.

She fell asleep . . . hoping to dream of home.

Instead, she saw herself walking beside a stream. A handsome prince appeared and took her hand.

"Please, don't leave me!" he begged. "Save me from this terrible spell."

"What spell?" Beauty replied.

But the prince didn't answer.

The next day, Beauty explored the castle.
In a big hall there were hundreds of portraits.

How curious,
it's the **prince**
from my dreams!

That night, Beauty and the Beast ate dinner together.

"Have you enjoyed your day? Do you like your bedroom? Have you got enough to eat?" asked the Beast.

"You're so kind. You can't be evil," replied Beauty. "Just very hairy."

Things went on like this for several days.

One night the Beast asked, **"Will you marry me?"**

"But I don't love you!" cried Beauty.

It made her sad to refuse the kind Beast, so she added, "You're a good person. Just very . . . um . . . beastly."

Every night, the Beast asked her to marry him. But Beauty was in love with her dream prince.

BOTANICAL ILLUSTRATI FOR BEGINNERS

The Beast saw that Beauty was unhappy.
She didn't want to mention the prince, so
she said, "I miss my family."

This was true. Mostly.

"Then you must visit them!" said the
Beast. "But you must also promise to return
within a week, or I will die without you."

Beauty's family were overjoyed to see her, and the week passed very quickly. But she never once dreamed of the prince.

At first she had wonderful dreams.

But then one night . . .

I dreamed my Beast was dead!

"What if it's true?" cried Beauty. She had to get back to the castle!

Beauty searched the castle from top to bottom.
Eventually she went down to the end of the
garden, and there she found the Beast.

"This is my fault!"

Beauty tried everything she could
to help him.

But nothing worked.

At last, in deep despair, she began to cry.

When her tears struck the Beast's body,

a marvellous thing happened . . .

He came back to life!

"I was dying because I thought you'd forgotten your promise," said the Beast. "But you returned! Will you **marry** me?"

"Oh yes, dear Beast!" Beauty cried.

Suddenly the Beast began to glow with a magical light. When the light faded, her prince stood before her!

"A cruel witch turned me into a beast," he explained. "I've been so lonely. But your true love has broken the spell."

Beauty and the prince were married.

The whole family came to live at the castle.

And they **all** lived **happily** ever after.

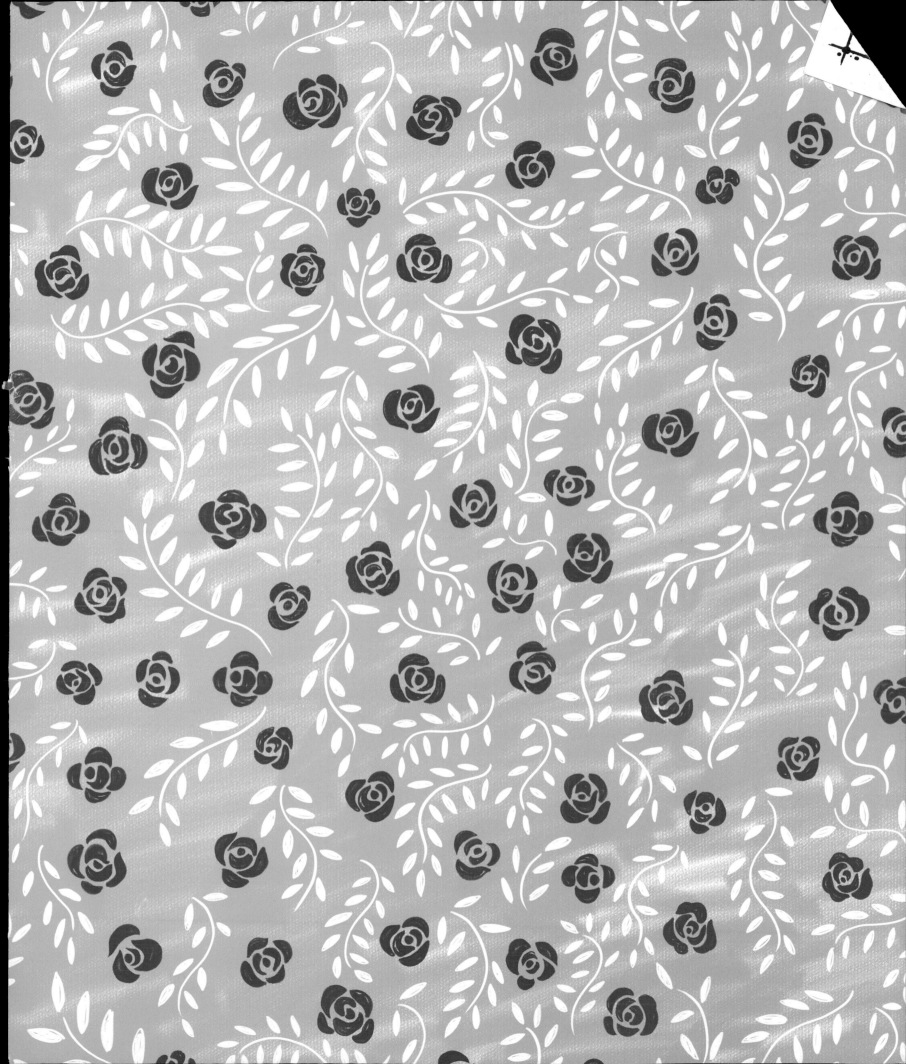

FAIRYTALE CLASSICS

are familiar, fun and friendly stories –
with a marvellously modern twist!

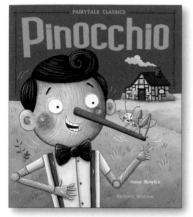

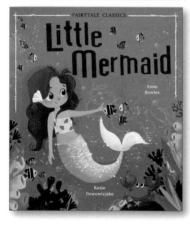

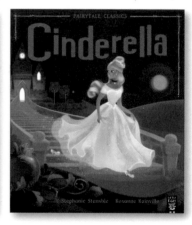

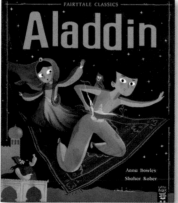

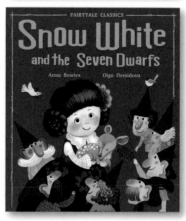

For information regarding any of the above titles
or for our catalogue, please contact us:
Little Tiger Press Ltd, 1 Coda Studios,
189 Munster Road, London SW6 6AW
Tel: 020 7385 6333 • E-mail: contact@littletiger.co.uk
www.littletiger.co.uk